Outside Time, Inside Time

Story by Carmel Reilly
Illustrations by Miriam Serafin

Contents

Chapter 1

Outside Time

"Outside time!" called Mum, walking into the living room.

I looked up from my desk in the corner of the room. "Great!" I said. "I'm just finishing my last maths question."

My sister Misha ran out from her bedroom and jumped up and down. "Outside time! Outside time!" she squealed.

“At last!” said Dad, getting up from where he had been working at the kitchen table.

“It’s lovely to see how popular our family walks are these days!” said Mum, smiling.

About a month ago, a virus started spreading around our city, making people sick. To stop us from catching the virus, we were all told to stay at home as much as possible, and to keep a distance from people we don't live with.

We're only allowed to leave our home for an hour of exercise each day. So, now we go out every afternoon when we've all finished our work. We call this "outside time", and it is the best part of our day.

“Are you ready to go, Sienna and Misha?” asked Dad, as he and Mum each put on a face mask.

“I am!” I said eagerly, grabbing the ball to take with us.

“Me, too,” giggled Misha.

Misha and I don’t need to wear face masks because we are kids. But Mum and Dad do.

As always, it felt amazing to be outside. The air smelled fresh, and everything was incredibly quiet. Our road is usually fairly busy, but these days there are hardly any cars driving around. Instead, the people we saw were walking, running and riding their bikes.

Even though all the adults and teenagers were wearing face masks, I still recognised a few of our neighbours. Many of them waved or said hello, even the ones we don't know very well.

Chapter 2

Kicking the Ball

We walked to the park, a couple of streets away from our apartment. The playground where Misha and I often went was closed now. This was to keep people from getting too close to one another, in case they passed on the virus.

Today, our family stuck together and kicked a ball around on the grass. I thought about my closest friend, Lewis. I wished he could come and kick the ball around with us, too. I really missed spending time with him.

Before heading back home, we went for a walk around the pond in the centre of the park.

"Outside time goes too quickly," said Misha, glumly, as we trudged along.

"I know," I sighed. "It's like time speeds up out here and when we go home it slows down! It's so boring being stuck inside so much."

But, actually, that afternoon I was looking forward to getting back home. Lewis and I had organised to have a video call and I was really excited about seeing him. We always had so much to talk about.

Chapter 3

Catching Up

Although Lewis and I saw each other every day in our online class, we didn't get to catch up properly like we usually did at school. We only got to talk to each other on video calls two or three times a week.

I clicked "connect" next to Lewis's name on the screen of my laptop. In seconds, his face appeared.

"Hi! What's up?" we both said at once.

When we had stopped laughing about both speaking at the same time, Lewis asked, "What have you been doing?"

"I've been to the park," I said. "What about you?"

Lewis told me he'd been helping his dad, who is a really good cook, in the kitchen at home. "One good thing about being stuck inside all day is that Dad is teaching me how to cook!" he said.

"I get bored having to stay inside so much," I said. "I don't think I want to learn to cook, but I would really like to find some other activities to do, apart from schoolwork."

"There are heaps of things you could do!" said Lewis, enthusiastically. "My cousin gave me some good ideas for games and crafts. I'll type them all out and email them to you."

"Thanks! That would be excellent," I said.

Just then, I had a thought. "There are probably lots of other people looking for extra activities to do," I said. "Maybe we could make an e-zine. It could be called *Things to Do When You're Stuck Inside*."

Lewis's eyes lit up. "I love that idea," he said.

Chapter 4

Things to Do When You're Stuck Inside

Lewis and I immediately started brainstorming ideas for our e-zine.

"Let's add some recipes and include reviews of the books we've been reading," Lewis exclaimed.

"Other people can contribute as well," I said. "Then we'll never run out of ideas."

"We can email it to friends and family," said Lewis.

"And what about printing a few copies as well, and leaving them around our neighbourhoods?" I suggested.

At dinner that night, I told my family about the e-zine.

"Can I put something in it?" asked Misha.

"Of course," I replied.

"I can show people how to make one of my finger puppets," Misha said excitedly.

"What will you do, Sienna?" Dad asked me.

"Lewis and I decided that I'm going to do most of the design," I said. "Maybe I'll put in some funny drawings, too."

"You're going to be busy," said Mum.

Chapter 5

Reaching Out

It took us a couple of weeks to put together the first e-zine, and Lewis and I were really happy with what we had done.

In the end, we emailed it to our friends, family and classmates. We also printed some copies that we left around our local neighbourhoods during outside time.

We started getting responses almost straight away. Our teacher, Mr Holt, emailed us to say that he loved reading it and couldn't wait for the next one.

My grandma said reading it made her feel less lonely, and she sent in a recipe for us to put in next time!

I think it's funny that we decided to make an e-zine filled with ideas for activities. It turns out that the activity I've enjoyed the most is making the e-zine!

And Lewis and I have decided that we'd like to keep doing it – even when we're no longer stuck inside.